# LOST and FOUND

## A Collection of Short Stories

## by
## Maria Savva

Published by:
Rose and Freedom Books
P.O. Box 55285
London N22 9EU
England, U.K.

A catalogue record of this book is available from the British Library

ISBN: 978-0-9928345-2-4

# Author's note

Thank you for choosing to read "Lost and Found". Most of these stories were written many years ago. In fact the only new story in the collection is "Boomerang", which was originally called "Lost and Found".

I decided to name the collection "Lost and Found" because I thought these stories had been lost. When I wrote them, back in the late '90s, I saved them on a floppy disk. I found the disk, which I had labelled "Short stories", a couple of years ago. I was quite excited when I found it as I had almost forgotten about these stories. I bought a device which connected by USB to my computer so that I could try to read the disk, but found that the disk had become corrupted so the stories were wiped off it. Only the titles could be read.

About a year ago I found typed copies of the stories in a drawer at home and after reading through them I chose a few to publish. I'd written the stories originally for writing competitions. In my early days as a writer, I used to enter a lot of short story competitions. I eventually won a competition with a story called "The Game of Life"; that story has been published in one of my earlier collections: "Delusion and Dreams".

It was wonderful to find these stories. They were in need of editing because my writing has changed quite a lot in the past twenty years. I rewrote some of the scenes and added different endings in some cases, but the stories remain true to the originals.

# Acknowledgements

I would like to thank the following amazing people for their help with this collection:

Bob Helle (editing).

Julie Aldridge and Darcia Helle (beta readers).

Kat at Aeternum Design (cover design).

# Contents:

# A Different World

'Hello, Mrs Johnson,' said Peter to the old lady sitting in front of him.

'Hello, dear.' She smiled even though her brow had been wrinkled into a frown only moments before.

Peter felt a burst of pride: being the reason someone smiled, even for a little while, made him feel much better about himself. He certainly wouldn't want to do this job for ever, but Mrs Johnson's smile gave his morale a much-needed boost.

Having just completed his studies to become a solicitor, Peter was finding it difficult to secure a training contract. The recession meant there were far fewer opportunities available. He'd been trying to get a contract for over three months. The job centre sent him to all sorts of courses to try to improve his skills, and the staff were now putting pressure on him to take any available employment. His adviser, Roxanne, had told him quite plainly, 'Mr Grace, I know you've studied to be a solicitor, but the reality is you haven't been able to find work for months. If you don't take the position we've suggested for you, I'm afraid you'll be forfeiting your right to benefits. You have to be seen to be actively seeking work.'

He'd protested, saying he *was* actively seeking work as a trainee solicitor, but Roxanne sneered and said, 'You can carry on doing that while you're working elsewhere.'

Roxanne peered down her nose at him, treating him as another statistic, an unemployed person who had to be found work to meet government targets. His dreams were unimportant.

Although overqualified, Peter had no alternative but to take the job they'd found for him.

'It's a lovely sunny day, isn't it?' said Mrs Johnson.

'Yes,' said Peter, nodding. He sighed to himself as he stood there. He'd studied for years but his ambitions had fallen by the wayside, it seemed.

'I was hoping I'd see you today,' she said happily. 'I wasn't sure if you'd be here. I made you some chocolate-chip muffins last night. Here you are.' The old woman held out a round tin —the kind that people only buy at Christmas; a biscuit selection-box.

'Thank you very much,' said Peter, taking the gift from her. 'How thoughtful of you.'

'You remind me of my son, Howard. He lives in South America, you know.'

'Oh, yes, I remember you telling me.'

'I hardly get to see him. I miss him so much.'

Peter sat next to her as she recounted stories about her son. He felt as though he knew Howard even though he'd never met him, having heard so many of Mrs Johnson's stories. Peter nodded and smiled and laughed in all the right places as he listened to Mrs Johnson reminisce. Having someone to talk to made the working day less tedious. It didn't matter that she repeated the same anecdotes each time they met; something in the repetition soothed Peter's mind.

The job was mundane. It required no thought, really. Most people walked by him as if he were invisible. The few like Mrs Johnson, helped to lift his spirits and made him feel appreciated. If nothing else, he kept her company and listened when no one else would. She sat in the same place every day, like a permanent fixture.

'I'll have to get on with my work now,' said Peter politely.

'Of course, dear. I mustn't keep you. Can I just say, I think you do a great job. We need people like you.'

A tear came to Peter's eye, unexpectedly, on hearing those words of reassurance. Since leaving university he'd gone from interview to interview and rejection letter to rejection letter. It wasn't often he heard any positive words.

Walking away from Mrs Johnson, he noticed Jack sitting in his usual spot. The old man appeared glum. Jack always looked sad: he had that type of face. Despair was stubbornly etched into his features.

Jack's life had not been easy. He'd told Peter about his days in the army; he'd served in the Second World War and seen many of his closest friends die before his eyes. Later he married, but became an alcoholic. He said his addiction to drink was caused by his inability to deal with the trauma of the war and the atrocities he'd witnessed; he drank to block it all out. His wife left him, unable to put up with his moods. He had three children but was no longer in contact with any of them. In the winter of his life, he found himself alone.

Peter made a point of stopping to speak to Jack whenever he saw him. This man, like Mrs Johnson, fitted in here. They were part of the scenery, but somehow Peter could tell they'd rather be anywhere else. They were victims of fate. Peter empathised; the past few months had been full of turmoil, constantly trying to prove his worth and being knocked down. In the weatherworn faces of Jack and Mrs Johnson, Peter saw a reflection of his own spirit. There was a connection that bound them and brought them closer. They were outsiders, forgotten by an uncaring world.

Peter approached the old man. 'Hello, Jack, how are you today?'

Jack peered up at him.

Peter never quite knew what mood Jack would be in. He changed from day to day, even from hour to hour. At times, he came across as relaxed and philosophical; at other times, though, he would be angry with the world.

'Hello, son.' He nodded at Peter. He did not appear to be in the mood to talk.

Peter continued with his work, thinking about the job application forms he needed to complete that evening.

The next day, Peter received a letter in the post. The frank on the envelope bore the name of the solicitors' firm where he'd been for an interview the week before. The initial burst of excitement was followed by the descent of gloom. In this moment, as he held the closed envelope, a million dreams swam around his head. He tried to stay positive: just because he'd been rejected a hundred times before, it didn't necessarily follow that this would be a rejection. Maybe those jobs simply weren't meant for him, but perhaps this one was.

Eventually, Peter sighed and decided to find out what the Fates had in store for him. Staring at the envelope wouldn't change the contents, it was only putting off the inevitable.

He fully expected to read the standard type of rejection letter, "We regret to inform you that we shall not be offering you the position, etc."

With jaded eyes, he began to read the letter. He caught his breath in surprise, and relief, when he saw it wasn't a rejection: he'd been offered a training contract.

Peter laughed out loud, overcome with joy, and incredulity. The next hour was spent on the phone to family and close friends, spreading the good news.

He handed in his resignation that same day and happily walked away from his old job. When he returned home, however, sorrow invaded his mind as he remembered Jack and Mrs Johnson. They'd been there for him as much as he'd been there for them lately. Who would listen to Mrs Johnson's stories now, and who'd talk to Jack? Peter felt selfish leaving them without even saying goodbye.

He'd be based on the other side of town in the solicitors' office, nearer to where he lived, so it was unlikely he'd see them again.

On the Sunday before he was due to start his training at the solicitors' firm, Peter made a special visit to where he used to work.

Walking through the entrance, he spotted Mrs Johnson immediately.

'Peter! Hello.' Her face brightened as soon as she set eyes on him.

The usual tug of Peter's heart strings was followed by a burst of melancholia, as he realised this might be the last time he would see her.

'Hello, Mrs Johnson. How are you?' He sat next to her.

'I'm very well, Peter. I spoke to Howard yesterday; he tells me it's winter in South America. He said he'd try to come and see me soon.'

'Oh, wow; that's great news. You must be pleased.'

'I am.' She smiled at him.

'I have some news for you, too,' said Peter. 'I've found another job.'

'Oh, you finally found work as a solicitor?'

'A trainee solicitor, yes.' He watched as she took a tissue from her handbag.

Her eyes filled with tears. 'I'll miss you, but it's for the best, Peter.'

Overcome by emotion, Peter held her hand and said, 'I wanted to say goodbye because I'm not sure if I'll be able to come here anymore. I'll be busy.'

Freeing her hand from his, she blinked away a tear and nodded. 'That's understandable, dear.'

He sat with her for a while longer as she updated him on her son's news, and then he said goodbye with a heavy heart.

Standing up, he glanced over at where Jack usually sat and was glad to see him there. As ever, he looked sad. Peter took a seat beside him and explained he would no longer be working there.

'Who's going to keep the place clean and tidy?' asked Jack, in a half-drunken slur. 'Who's going to pick up all the litter?'

'They'll employ a new street cleaner soon, Jack. Don't worry,' he soothed, patting the old man on the back.

As Peter walked away towards the gates, he could not help turning around to take in the surroundings one final time. He felt privileged to have been a part of this little world. The memory of this park would forever remain in his heart; it was Mrs Johnson's and Jack's whole world. He knew he would never forget them.

# An Innocent Man

Somehow, they'd ended up here, with Oliver on trial for assault. Dean's arm was badly wounded as a result of being struck with a broken beer bottle.

Oliver told the court he'd acted in self-defence.

Although Elizabeth hadn't been present on the day in question, there was no doubt in her mind that he was telling the truth.

The months leading up to the trial were stressful, and now the reality of the day in court proved intolerable. The evidence was based on hearsay as far as she could tell. Elizabeth felt helpless knowing she couldn't do anything to stop the trial, to prevent an innocent man being convicted.

Oliver's face didn't give away his thoughts, but Elizabeth knew that behind the steely facade he must harbour deep pain at the injustice.

'I held out the bottle in front of me because he was going to punch me,' explained Oliver from his position in the witness box. 'He was so drunk, but more than that, he struck me as crazy—out of control. Angry. I have no idea why he was angry: I didn't do anything to him. The beer bottle broke when he ran towards me to attack me; it bashed against the side of the bar, I think, and then it cut his arm.'

Elizabeth's tears threatened to fall as Oliver gave evidence, but she kept her emotions in check, not wanting Dean to see her discomposure. Inwardly, she was willing Oliver on.

Her stomach turned as she thought of Dean. Twice the size of the accused, his previous convictions for robbery and assault read like a shopping list. This was Oliver's first time in court.

'I was in the pub enjoying the evening,' Oliver explained. 'We were celebrating a friend's birthday. That man,'—he pointed to Dean—'came up to me, from out of nowhere, and started picking a fight.'

Elizabeth watched on, silently. Oliver looked so small standing there. Envisioning the altercation between Dean and Oliver, it seemed obvious to her that Oliver would have been afraid. Surely the jury would draw the same conclusion.

Having thought it over, again and again, she couldn't comprehend why the police arrested Oliver rather than Dean, but here he was, being charged with grievous bodily harm. The likelihood was he'd be sent to prison for years, if convicted.

Her torturous thoughts were overpowering as she watched this young man pleading to be believed. If only she could stand up and say a few words in his defence, shake off this sense of culpability. A familiar feeling of shame taunted her: the silence affirmed her cowardice. Was she to blame? If only she'd said something before... She hadn't, and she wouldn't now; of that much she was certain.

Catching Oliver's eye briefly, Elizabeth could almost see the resentment. Inner demons screamed and mocked her.

She looked away. *I wish I'd been there that night*; that thought had continually nagged her over the past few months, but another always prevailed: *What would I have done? Nothing.*

Elizabeth fiddled with her wedding ring, ashamed and unable to meet Oliver's dejected gaze.

The jury didn't take long to reach a "not guilty" verdict. It was unanimous. Oliver's face brightened and Elizabeth couldn't help smiling.

Dean stood up, red-faced. 'You call that justice!'

Elizabeth, seated beside him, squirmed as he turned towards her and caught the remains of her smile as it dwindled. His eyes were full of venom. His stare burned through her.

As she watched him storm out of the courtroom, Elizabeth shivered. Standing up, and picking up her handbag with a trembling hand, she hesitated before walking towards the exit; he'd probably be waiting outside the courtroom, hatred still raging in his eyes.

Ironically, as much as she'd been praying for Oliver, it would have been easier for her if it had been a guilty verdict: at least then Dean might be in a good mood. She couldn't remember the last time he'd been in a good mood in their five years of marriage. She prayed he wouldn't get drunk tonight and hit her like he usually did.

# Boomerang

One Wednesday, a week or so before Christmas, Tiffany's mother deliberately abandoned her in a large department store.

Helen didn't want to look after Tiffany anymore but felt sure that someone would find her and take care of her.

Only a couple of weeks earlier, Helen had been watching a television programme about couples who couldn't have children. She'd watched the programme in disbelief, arguing with the couples on the television screen as if they were in the room: 'Oh, so you really want to have a baby, yeah? Well, you can forget about ever bloody sleeping again. Count yourself lucky: you don't have to change nappies every five minutes and be kept awake by annoying screams! Not to mention not being able to find time to have a shower or even change your clothes or do your hair... You won't be looking like that in a few months' time if you've got a baby. You'll be looking like me.'

The couples on the documentary cried openly and bemoaned their fate. Some had tried IVF, others opted for adoption. Helen ended up switching off the television after shouting 'clueless idiots!' at the screen.

One thing she knew for certain when she left three-year-old Tiffany in the department store, was that there were childless couples everywhere praying for a child like Tiffany.

Tiffany's father, Ronan, left home when she was just a year old. He'd stood at the front door, a blank expression on his face, and said, 'I ain't cut out to be a dad. I'm too young... Too independent. I need my freedom.'

Helen hadn't seen him since, but heard through the grapevine that he'd moved to Australia and was living with another woman.

Helen and Ronan used to talk about travelling the world together. They'd even planned to visit Australia. All the talk of travel stopped after she became pregnant.

She'd booked an appointment at the local clinic to have an abortion. Her own mother had eight children and, as the eldest, Helen was always called upon to help out; consequently, she swore never to have children of her own.

When Ronan found the appointment card, they'd argued. He said abortion was akin to murder: 'Leave it to me, Helen. I want this baby. I'll take care of it. Believe me, once you see the child you'll want it too. It's ours.' His eyes were gleaming as he spoke.

Feeling supported by the man she loved, Helen had slowly warmed to the idea.

The pregnancy went quite smoothly. The real problems only began after Tiffany was born. Helen suffered postnatal depression, meaning that Ronan took on most of the responsibility. He was often in a bad mood, ostensibly resenting his new role.

A couple of months after Tiffany was born, he marched Helen to their GP to get some antidepressants.

It wasn't long before she began to feel controlled by the pills, unable to experience any emotions fully—neither happiness nor sadness. There were no extremes, just a measured dose that permitted her to live life at a safe distance from reality; it felt almost as if she were looking in on the world as a spectator who lacked the ability or freedom to join in, only getting so far before the invisible reins restrained her.

Without consulting Ronan, she made the decision to stop taking the pills. The arguments resumed.

When Ronan left, life became insufferable for Helen. Daily tasks—like getting out of bed, cooking, interacting with other people—led to exhaustion. It seemed to her that Tiffany required constant attention.

She'd lost touch with her family; her mother had never liked Ronan and this had soured Helen's relationship with her. She did think of contacting her mother after Ronan left, but couldn't go through with it, feeling too ashamed to ask for help.

As the days turned to weeks, Helen's bitterness towards Tiffany grew: she increasingly saw her as a burden. She contemplated giving the child up for adoption, but that would mean admitting she was a bad mother. Each day she faced a battle between pride and sanity.

Sometimes, when Tiffany cried, Helen would join in. Helen spent hours crying.

One evening, on opening the bathroom cabinet, she saw the antidepressants. The temptation was there to consume the rest of the bottle in one go: there were around forty tablets left. Would that be deadly enough?

She took the packet out of the cabinet and stood staring at herself in the mirror for a good few minutes. *What would Ronan think of me if he saw me like this?* The thought came unexpectedly. Her desire to see him suddenly became paramount.

Recalling Ronan's parting words, and following endless nights of disrupted sleep with Tiffany screaming at all hours, Helen understood what he'd meant about needing freedom.

The world she inhabited felt like a prison. It was an ongoing struggle just trying to fit in. She couldn't relate to the other mothers at the toddler group she attended; they invariably fussed over their children and openly displayed their affection with hugs and kisses. To Helen, Tiffany was nothing but a hindrance.

Helen had—on at least two occasions in the past six months—come close to harming the child.

One night, she contemplated suffocating Tiffany. She held a pillow over her bed, thinking *it's for the best, it's for the best*. Fortunately, she didn't go through with it, avoiding what could have been a living nightmare.

Despite deeply regretting that incident, a few weeks later she'd ground down twenty paracetamol tablets and added the powder to the child's juice bottle. Moments before handing the bottle to Tiffany, the voice of conscience drowned out all other thoughts: *What am I doing?*

Exhausted and increasingly unstable, Helen decided the girl would be better off with someone else. Her intention had never been to kill Tiffany, just rid herself of the responsibility; however, her mind ticked like a time bomb that threatened to explode.

She envied all the women she'd known at school who didn't have children. Many of them had jobs and careers. Whenever their paths crossed in the street, those women would coo at little Tiffany. 'You're so lucky,' they would say. Helen wished she could swap lives with them.

The idea of having "freedom" gradually became more like a dream—unattainable. She'd never be free with this child demanding so much, sucking out all of her energy.

Lying awake in bed one night, staring at the ceiling at 3 a.m., after struggling to get Tiffany to sleep for the fifth night in a row, she began to devise a plan.

Twice, recently, she'd come close to losing Tiffany in crowds whilst out shopping. Since she now preferred walking rather than sitting in a pram, the toddler often ran alongside her. Helen sometimes prayed her daughter would be snatched away or simply vanish into the crowd. Guilt weighed heavily on her mind after thinking such things, but when tears or a tantrum came she would once more yearn to be free.

The first time Tiffany nearly got lost, Helen had been getting off a bus when the child ran back inside. A do-gooder on the bus alerted the driver. Helen's reticence in taking Tiffany's hand was interpreted by some of the passengers as a reaction caused by shock. Strangers on the bus were quick to comfort her: 'Don't worry, love; she's safe with her mummy now.'

One woman even gave her a hug and said, 'You poor thing; that must have been terrifying. It wasn't your fault.'

The second time she nearly lost her was at the local convenience store. Tiffany had run along the freezer aisle while Helen was at the till; Helen willed the shop assistant to hurry up and total up the goods, intending to leave the store without Tiffany.

As she rushed to pack the shopping into her car boot, familiar and jarring screams sounded close behind. She felt a tap on her shoulder.

The tall, bearded, shop manager smiled and said, 'I think you may have forgotten something.' He patted Tiffany on the head.

'Oh... er... yes, thank you,' muttered Helen, putting on a cheery smile.

'Happens all the time, don't worry,' said the manager.

Those words: *happens all the time,* were now helping to formulate a plan. The words of the woman on the bus: 'It wasn't your fault', also resonated. Children had been known to get lost in crowds. She decided to deliberately lose Tiffany in a store in the next town. Someone would find her and be a better parent than she could ever be. A smile—her first true smile in years—spread across her lips. *Freedom.* It was no longer such an impossible dream.

Helen pulled Tiffany by the arm as they walked along the busy street. 'Come on,' she urged.

'I'm tired, Mummy. Pick me up.'

'No!' she squealed in response. *Tired! Huh! You're tired? You're the one who kept me awake all night.*

The street was unfamiliar, three miles from home. Christmas shoppers were out in force searching for last-minute bargains. *She could easily get lost in this crowd...*

But Helen didn't want the child to end up with someone who might harm her.

A shop window display came into view: snow, a Christmas tree, colourful lights, reindeer. A large department store. *Perfect.*

On entering through the double doors into the store, the welcoming warmth hit Helen in contrast to the freezing temperatures outside. She took this as a good omen, a reassurance that she'd made the right decision. A spark of joy exploded like a firework in her mind: soon she'd be free. She'd find Ronan and they could be happy again.

A mutual friend, Russell, still kept in touch with Ronan and knew his address. The dream beckoned.

They took the escalator to the first floor and the toy department. Helen let go of Tiffany's hand. 'Go and play with the toys,' she mumbled.

The three-year-old ran over to a large teddy bear that was practically the same size as her. 'Mummy, Mummy! Look! Can I have it?'

Another mother, pushing a pram, noticed her. 'Just like my kids,' the woman said, smiling knowingly. 'They want all the toys in the shop!'

Helen forced a smile.

When Tiffany turned around to pick up the teddy bear, Helen saw a chance to escape and began to run towards the escalator.

At the double-door exit, she stood outside and found that her feet refused to move any further. It was almost as if she'd woken up from a long delusional sleep. *Oh my God!* She covered her face with both hands. *How could I even have considered...?* As she wiped away a stray tear, she exclaimed, 'I can't do this!'

A couple of passersby glanced over at her, apparently wondering if she needed help. She was too preoccupied with inner turmoil to notice their stares.

Praying Tiffany was safe, she re-entered the store. Remorse overwhelmed her as she suddenly became aware that none of this was Tiffany's fault. If anything, Ronan was to blame.

As she hurried towards the escalator, her mobile phone vibrated in her pocket. Absent-mindedly, she took out the phone. The caller ID caught her eye: *Ronan*. His name flashed on the display. *It can't be.* In a daze, she clicked to accept the call.

'Hi hon, I'm at the flat. Where are you? I've missed you,' came the familiar voice.

It was the first contact in just under two years. Helen didn't respond immediately, stunned at how the sound of his voice brought to mind long-forgotten memories.

'Helen?'

'What d'you want?' she managed to ask.

'I want you... You and Tiff. I'm so sorry. I made a mistake. The single life ain't all it's cracked up to be.'

'Um... I have to go. Tiff needs me.'

'Okay, I'll crash out here for a while until you get back. Massive headache, jet lag. See you later. Love you.'

*Love you.* The words resounded in her head, bringing a warmth that soothed. This was the answer. Ronan had returned and he'd take care of her and Tiffany. She shook her head: *What am I thinking?*

She headed to the toy department, trying to dispel all thoughts of her errant ex-boyfriend, too anxious to think about him now as concern for the toddler took precedence.

Her eyes scanned the toy department. Calling out 'Tiffany! Tiff, where are you?', Helen practically ransacked the store, throwing teddy bears and other toys aside.

A sales assistant approached. 'Are you okay, Madam?'

'No, um... I've lost my daughter... She's only three.' Tears pricked Helen's eyes.

The sales assistant smiled. 'Oh. Yes, we found a little girl wandering around alone a few minutes ago. She had a bit of an accident. Wet herself. One of my colleagues took her to the toilets. I'll go and find them.'

Helen placed a hand over her mouth, hating herself. She followed the shop assistant.

As they walked towards the toilets, a tall blonde woman exited holding Tiffany's hand. Tiffany was cradling the large teddy bear that she'd been playing with earlier.

'Mummy! Mummy!'

'Tiffany, oh, Tiff, I'm so sorry.'

'We found her in the store calling out for you,' explained the blonde woman. 'We had to change her clothes, but don't worry, you can keep the new ones. I've put her other clothes in a bag for you.' The woman held out a plastic bag and Helen took it.

'Thank you,' said Helen through tears.

'We've given her the teddy as a Christmas present,' continued the woman.

'No, I—'

The woman waved a hand to dismiss her protest. 'We'd love her to have it. I'm just glad we've found you now.'

Helen hugged her daughter when the shop assistants had departed, and for the first time she felt something more than loathing towards the child.

Her thoughts turned to Ronan. He'd be at the flat now. *Why didn't I change the locks when he left?* She pondered the hours and days she'd spent wishing he would return to her life. Now he was back, she could not decide whether it was a good thing or a bad thing.

Her emotions were all over the place. One minute, she couldn't wait to return to the flat and lose herself in his arms, leave behind the nightmarish time she'd spent alone with Tiffany; then she'd find herself cursing the invading thoughts, questioning her sanity, and doubting she could ever trust him after what he'd done. He'd left them before, he could do it again. Despite everything, she longed to believe that he'd learned a lesson and that he meant it when he said he wanted them back.

Sitting on the bus, halfway home, it occurred to Helen that her mother's house was not far away. If she got off at the next stop it would only take a minute or two to get there. With all the fluctuating thoughts that were driving her mad, perhaps she needed someone to take the strain, someone to help her decide what she should do. Maybe she could leave Tiffany at her mother's house and go to see Ronan alone; it would be easier for them to talk without distraction.

In a spur-of-the-moment decision, she took Tiffany's hand and got off the bus. She stood at the bus stop staring in the direction of her mother's house, wondering if she could muster the courage to proceed. The last time she'd seen her mother, or any of her siblings, was over three years ago. None of them had even met Tiffany.

Tiffany began to walk ahead, pulling Helen forward and distracting her from her reverie.

'We... We're going to see your grandma, okay, Tiff?'

'Granma. Who's Granma?'

'My mum.'

'You can't have a mum, silly. You are old.'

'I do have a mum,' she replied, tears welling in her eyes. The time that had passed between them now seemed like a chasm. They were little more than strangers. Once again, she inwardly cursed Ronan for distancing her from her family. Why had she let so much time pass between them? There was no excuse for staying away from them for so long when Ronan was out of the picture. Feeling a chill, she pulled her coat closer around her, realising she wasn't the only one who hadn't tried to make contact: none of her sisters or brothers had made any attempt to get in touch, and her mother had not once picked up a phone to talk to her.

Helen made an effort to think positively. This was her family; surely they could let bygones be bygones, and start over.

Soon, they approached the familiar pink gate. Pink. Helen caught her breath. It had been her idea to paint the gate pink when they decorated the house. The fact that it remained the same had to count for something. They could easily have repainted it if they hated her as she often suspected they did.

Taking a deep breath, she pulled open the gate and walked towards the front door. Tiffany ran alongside.

Helen rang the doorbell and waited.

A middle-aged man opened the door. He was tall, dark-haired. He looked like a man in an old photo she'd seen somewhere. Slowly her memory returned. She brought a hand up to cover her mouth. *He's back?*

'Can I help you?' he asked gruffly.

'It's me. Helen.'

He shrugged and then froze momentarily.

She noticed as he visibly attempted to hide his discomposure.

'Your mum's not in. She's at work.'

'You came back.' The words, full of disbelief, sprang from her lips as she tried to make sense of the situation.

He sighed. 'Your mum was in a right state after you left. Kids all over the place, no one to help. She called me and I came back. Did the right thing. She told me you left, said you were selfish: found a fella and left her to cope on her own.'

Helen stood open-mouthed, unable to believe what she was hearing.

'I know I'm not faultless,' he continued. 'God knows I wasn't here for her for years, and she did her best. But when it came down to it, when she needed me most, I came through. You should be ashamed of yourself, leaving your mother and all your brothers and sisters for some jerk. She told me he was no good for you, but you didn't listen to her.' He appeared to only just notice Tiffany, who was peering up at him, her body partially hidden behind the large teddy bear she was cuddling. 'What's happened now, eh? Has he left you and you need her help, or something?'

Helen hung her head, not wanting him to see the tears threatening to fall. 'I should come back when Mum's here,' was all she managed to say. She took Tiffany by the hand.

'Don't bother; you're not welcome,' said her father as he walked into the house and slammed the door behind him.

Suppressing a waterfall of tears, Helen somehow made it back to her flat.

The unexpected meeting with her estranged father had caused a well of unresolved pain to burst open. He'd left home when she was just eleven years old. Somehow, he'd returned and been forgiven by her mother despite the years of hell he'd put her through; despite the fact he'd deserted the family when the children were all so young.

She remembered her father as a man who was always angry, regularly punishing the children for things that were not their fault. He'd left home one day without warning; the rumours were that he was living with a woman and that she was pregnant.

Helen had helped look after her siblings while her mother spent most of the time crying and screaming, lamenting how unfair life was. When she'd met Ronan, her mother discouraged the relationship: Helen thought it was a ploy to keep her at home to help with the children. Ronan had said, 'Your dad left her for another woman, so it's not surprising she doesn't trust men. She doesn't want to see you get hurt, but you can't let her fear stop you living your life.'

Those words ran through Helen's mind occasionally, during the years that Ronan was away. Whenever they did, a yearning to see her mother would surface; a deep-rooted regret would grip her as she repeatedly wondered, *Why didn't I listen to Mum?* Now though, her world had been tipped upside down and she didn't know what to think.

As she walked into the flat and closed the front door she felt like a hypocrite: she was hating her mother for taking her father back and yet she was contemplating doing the same thing and forgiving Ronan.

There was a sound from the kitchen; the kettle boiling. The clink of a cup and spoon followed.

She approached trepidatiously and stood watching Ronan from the kitchen doorway. He threw a teaspoon into the sink.

As he turned around, their eyes met.

'Helen! Oh my God! Wow! It's so good to see you!' he said running towards her, picking her up, and twirling her around.

Her feet hit the chair next to the table. 'Ow, put me down.'

He did, and she leaned over to rub her ankles where they'd bashed into the chair.

'Sorry,' he said. 'I'm just so happy to see you.'

'Your voice sounds different. You sound Australian.'

31

'It's hard not to pick up the accent over there. I was living with a... someone who speaks with an Australian accent. It must've rubbed off.'

'Why are you here?' she asked stiffly, arms crossed.

He couldn't meet her eyes and appeared perturbed, as if he'd not expected this kind of reaction. 'Wait a minute,' he said excitedly.

She shook her head as he hurried past.

He soon returned, with a package in one hand and Tiffany perched on his hip. 'She's beautiful. Give me a chance to make it up to you. I should never have left.' He handed the package to Helen.

'What is it?' she asked, frowning.

'Open it and see.'

She tore the bright green paper and pulled out a wooden object. 'A boomerang? Very original. Is that the only souvenir they have in Australia?'

'I got a boomerang because, well, I left and I came back. It's symbolic: a peace offering really, and my promise that I won't leave you. After all, boomerangs always come back, right? You can't get rid of me.' He grinned and lifted Tiffany high above his head.

The child responded with squeals of delight, and for a moment Helen's heartache and pain became a distant whisper, no longer possessing any power. She stared at her daughter so relaxed in her father's arms. *Maybe this could work*, she mused.

An image of her own father's face, full of disdain, came to mind. 'How can I trust you?' she said.

'I know, I know; I really regret leaving. I should never have gone, but I've learned my lesson. I promise I won't let you down.'

Helen beheld the perfect picture: a father and child, both happy and smiling.

She walked into the living room.

'I'm not expecting miracles, Helen,' said Ronan, putting the child down and following her.

They both sat on the sofa while Tiffany played with her new teddy bear on the other side of the room.

'Just let me stay for a while. I want to get to know my little girl.' He took Helen's hand in his. 'And, me and you; we deserve another chance, don't we?'

'Do you have any idea how hard it's been for me?' she said, unable to stem the flow of tears any longer.

'Please don't cry; I'm here now. We'll sort it out.' He gave her a tissue and wrapped his arms around her.

His embrace evoked nostalgia for a time when life had been easier.

'If you think back to when I left,' he began, 'can you remember how stressed out we both were?'

She listened to his words as they reverberated off his chest, and closed her eyes. She didn't care what he was saying; for now, she just needed to know that he was there and would stay. 'Promise you won't leave me again.'

'I left because it was so hard. The baby was so small and I was responsible because you couldn't cope. Remember you were depressed? Everything was left to me, and I was just not ready to be a dad.'

Her tranquillity dissipated on hearing those words. He was not taking responsibility for his actions. Anger began to bubble below the surface. She yearned to hold on to this picture-perfect ending for her family, but how could she base it on half-truths?

'It wasn't only my fault, you know?' She pulled away from him and wiped her eyes. 'You left me when I was depressed. What does that make you?'

'I know, I know. But I couldn't cope, either.'

She stood up. 'I was depressed, and you left me to bring up a child with no help from anyone.'

33

'I can't change what I did.' He stood up to face her. 'I can try to make things right, though.'

'What have you been doing since you left?' she asked, arms folded. 'I heard you met someone else.'

He avoided her eyes. 'It was just a fling. I was missing you. I met her in a bar; we dated for a while, but it's over now.'

'What? She dumped you? Is that why you're back?'

'No. No. It's nothing like that. I left her. I couldn't stop thinking about you and Tiff. I knew I'd made a mistake.'

Helen took a seat on the sofa.

Ronan joined her. 'So, can I stay?'

She managed a half-smile, through tears. Shrugging, she nodded. 'For a while. We'll see how it goes.'

'Thank you!' He hugged her.

She immersed herself in the security of his embrace.

'Helen, I need to ask you a favour.' He leaned back on the sofa.

'Okay,' she said, wiping the final few tears from her cheeks.

'I met a bloke, Oscar, in Australia and we became great friends. His sister Gina is going to come to England next week to look for work and lodgings, and he asked me if she could stay with me. I couldn't say no because, once, I found myself homeless when I was in Oz, and he let me sleep on his sofa until I got back on my feet. She'd only need to stay until she finds somewhere else; what'd'ya say?'

'Um... It's only a one-bed flat. Where would she sleep?'

'I can sleep on the sofa. She can share with you. She's a nice girl. I think you'd like her.'

'I don't know.'

'Oh, come on, Helen.'

'Maybe she can stay for a few days—'

'You're a star! I'll go and e-mail her... I mean, I'll let Ozzie know.' He stood up.

34

'Who's Ozzie?' she asked.

'Her brother.'

'Didn't you say his name is Oscar?'

'Yeah, we call him Ozzie, though.'

'We?'

'*We*, as in his friends.'

Ronan logged into the PC in the bedroom. Being in the flat after so long made him uneasy. Helen was unpredictable. The place smelled of babies' nappies. Helen didn't smell all that great either. He wrinkled his nose as he thought of it. She looked so bedraggled, too. She seemed to have aged ten years in the past two.

As Ronan began to compose an e-mail, he wished he could Skype instead—he missed Gina—but that would be too dangerous. If Helen came in and saw him talking to her, she'd no doubt put two and two together.

**Hi Gina, I've arrived in the UK. Back at my old flat. My ex has agreed you can stay here until we find somewhere else. By the way, I had to pretend that me and her are giving it another try. No choice really because I don't have anywhere else to stay. My parents threw me out years ago, as I told you. We'll stay with Helen for a little while. I have to apologise in advance for the state of the place. Helen has completely let herself go since I last saw her and she hasn't made much of an effort with the flat either. And we have to put up with a toddler. Remember I told you the reason I left her was because she had a kid with another man? Well, he doesn't seem to want anything to do with her or the kid either. Best not to mention any of that when you're here. Keep the conversation to a minimum. Between me and you, I**

think her mental health has deteriorated too. She doesn't make much sense. We can stay here for as long as we can blag it. I'll try to find a job then we can rent somewhere together, I'll just tell her it wasn't working out, or something.

Love you and miss you, yours forever Ronan xxx

# What's Left Unsaid

Sandra's eyes were drawn to the beautiful card with red roses on the front. "Happy Valentine's Day" were the words above the picture. A plain but romantic statement. The familiar pang of jealousy taunted her, but she told herself to be strong. Jim promised he would be breaking up with Polly this weekend: the card was obviously just a token; something to cover up the lies until he found the courage to tell the truth.

Sandra and Jim had been seeing each other for three months now. They met in the staff room at work. He'd only just started working at the company. She'd felt an instant attraction to him, and the first thing she said was, 'I don't remember seeing you around here before, and I always remember a handsome face.'

He'd replied with, 'Mine must be ugly then.'

That had broken the ice, and after he introduced himself they'd chatted over a cup of tea.

She noticed he wasn't wearing a wedding ring and found herself telling him she was unhappy in her marriage. He never mentioned Polly.

They'd gone out for dinner that evening and ended up in a passionate embrace in the restaurant toilets.

Jim confessed the next day at work that he was married but said that he and his wife had grown apart. 'I think it's good timing that we've met now because we're both in bad relationships. We can do something about it,' he'd said.

Over the next few weeks, they spent a lot of time together and even went to each other's houses. Sandra introduced him to her husband, Fred, as a colleague from work. Jim introduced her to his wife, Polly. Fred and Polly didn't seem to suspect a thing. Fred suggested they all fly out on a city-break weekend to Paris. While there, Jim and Sandra found time to sneak away when their partners were sleeping, to spend time together in the romantic city.

Sandra had been disappointed when Jim said he was going to Spain with Polly for Valentine's weekend.

'We should be spending Valentine's Day together, Jim. It's you I love, not Fred. Why don't we tell them?'

'Be patient, Sandra; I'm taking her away so I can break up with her properly. I'm trying to avoid a bitter break-up. After all, we have kids together. I want to be able to explain my reasons to her.'

'What? About you and me, you mean?' asked Sandra.

Jim knitted his brow. 'No, I don't think that's necessary. She'll find out about us sooner or later, but I'd rather not tell her we were seeing each other behind her back.'

'Makes sense,' said Sandra shrugging. 'I suppose I'll have to think of the best way to tell Fred too.'

So here she was, in Jim and Polly's kitchen. She'd been asked by Polly, ironically, to keep an eye on the house while they were in Spain. 'Can you come over twice a day and feed the cat, please?' she'd said.

Polly gushed with excitement when talking about the Valentine's trip; it made Sandra question her morals. She'd put it to the back of her mind and agreed to feed the cat, holding on to the hope that soon all the sneaking around would be over.

Sandra had opened the drawer to retrieve the can opener when she came across the Valentine's card. It struck her as an odd place to keep a card, especially as it was practically hidden under everything in the drawer; perhaps it was meant to be hidden. Maybe this wasn't a card from Jim to Polly, but from Polly to Jim, and he'd not wanted it so had stashed it away out of sight: she preferred to believe that.

Curiosity made her take the card out of the drawer. As she began to read it, the colour drained from her cheeks. She had to sit down.

After taking a few deep breaths, she stood up and walked over to the sink to pour herself a glass of water. How could this be? It couldn't be true. She thought of Jim and suddenly saw it for what it was: an affair—something to pass the time and add a bit of excitement to what had become a routine existence. She didn't want to lose Fred, felt almost as if she'd woken up from a deep sleep. The Valentine's card made her appreciate her marriage. She'd been married to Fred for twenty years and they adored their three children, who'd all grown up and left home.

Did he know? Had he somehow found out about the affair, and was this his way of dealing with it?

Sandra sat at the kitchen table and picked up the Valentine's card, reading it over one more time, *"Dearest Polly, you mean the world to me, I am counting the days until we can be together. All my love, Fred xx"*

Fred and Polly. She'd never have guessed.

Just then, the front door opened. Jim and Polly were back from their weekend break.

Sandra stood up and composed herself, then scrabbled towards the drawer and replaced the Valentine's card where she'd found it.

'Sandra, hello,' Polly said brightly on entering the kitchen. 'Thank you so much for feeding Rusty.' Leaning over, she stroked the large tabby cat.

'It was no problem at all,' said Sandra. 'Did you have a nice break?'

'We had a wonderful time,' said Polly, 'and it's made us realise how much we love each other.'

Jim entered the room and put an arm around his wife.

'We've decided to renew our vows,' continued Polly, beaming. Her teeth appeared very white set off against her freshly tanned skin.

Sandra looked at Jim, eyebrows raised.

'Yes,' he said, nodding. 'Sometimes it's easy to lose sight of the fact that the person you really love is right there in front of you. Temptation is always there, but Polly and I have been together through thick and thin for years. That has to count for something.'

Polly gave him a kiss on the cheek and picked up her suitcase. 'I'm going to go and take the bags upstairs. Jim, make a cup of tea for Sandra; we can show her our photos.'

Polly floated out of the room.

Sandra's emotions were being batted back and forth. On hearing Jim and Polly were renewing their vows, desolation took hold. The desire to save her marriage disappeared and was replaced with the need for her lover's attention.

'P-please tell me that what you just said was a load of bullshit,' she said to Jim, arms folded.

'Please sit down, Sandra; I'll explain.'

She sighed and sat opposite him at the kitchen table.

Looking up at the ceiling, as if trying to find the right words, he said, 'Getting away from everything with Polly helped me see things from a different angle. We... We love each other.'

'But... But you said you loved me.'

Jim exhaled loudly. 'Please hear me out. I can't leave her. If I'm honest, I don't think I ever intended to leave her. What happened between *us* was like a cry for help. I thought I was going to lose her. I'd been neglecting her, and we kept having arguments about the littlest things. I needed someone to comfort me, I suppose, and you were there.'

'Charming,' said Sandra, rolling her eyes.

'I'm not saying you didn't mean anything to me, but—'

'I happened to be available, and gullible.'

40

He shook his head, 'It's never that black and white, Sandra.'

'You lied to me from the start.'

Jim glanced at the kitchen door, apparently concerned Polly would hear them. He lowered his voice and said, 'I have to give my marriage a chance. I'm sorry.'

Standing up, Sandra walked over to the drawer where she'd found the Valentine's card. 'Fine, but you should know that Polly hasn't been a hundred per cent honest with you. She's been having an affair with my husband!'

'I know,' said Jim.

Sandra frowned. 'You knew?'

'Yes, I knew.' He shrugged. 'I guess that's why I slept with you. I suppose I saw it as a kind of revenge.'

'But... But—'

'I'm sorry, Sandra. I deliberately started an affair with you to try to get back at Polly. She found out, which is why we decided to go away and talk things through.'

Sandra gulped. 'She knows about me and you?'

'Yes. Sorry. Polly and I will be retiring to Spain. I won't be around much longer. I'm really sorry for all the lies.'

'You were using me.'

He stood up, as if to indicate the discussion was over. 'You're not exactly innocent. You were cheating on your husband, remember.'

'Yes, and what happens to him, hey? Polly used him too. You're two peas in a pod. You deserve each other.'

'Why don't you patch up your relationship with Fred?'

'What? How can I do that now, knowing what I know?'

'Don't forget, you were having an affair too.'

She sneered and left the house, not wanting to see Polly.

When she arrived home, Sandra found Fred sitting on his favourite armchair watching television. She'd never have

41

guessed he'd be capable of having an affair: he seemed forever glued to his armchair, viewing an endless array of sports programmes, or documentaries about wildlife or gardening.

She tried, in vain, to drag back the feelings that had surfaced when she'd read the Valentine's card he'd sent to Polly, but all she could muster was indifference.

'Hello, love,' said Fred, finally noticing her standing by the living room door. 'You couldn't make us a cup of tea, could you?'

'Okay.'

Life had resumed to what it was before his affair and before hers. They'd been together for so many years, a few more wouldn't hurt. He'd no doubt be upset when Polly told him that she'd decided to stay with Jim. Maybe it would teach him a lesson, make him appreciate their relationship more. Perhaps he'd have another affair. She might too. For now, life would go on under the shadow of what was left unsaid.

# Office Gossip

When Steve stepped out of his office, Linda and Cathy looked up from their computer screens and stared goggle-eyed. Ever since he joined the company, two weeks ago, the secretaries had been constantly vying for his attention.

'Oh no!' exclaimed Linda, standing up as soon as he walked into the room. 'I've spilt my coffee.'

'There are some paper towels in there, I think,' said Steve, pointing to the staff kitchen.

'Thanks,' purred Linda, brushing past him suggestively on her way out of the room.

Cathy began to cough. 'Uh... uh... I need some water,' she spluttered.

The water cooler was directly behind Steve.

His secretary, Julie, stood up and poured a cup of water for Cathy.

'Oh... thanks.' Cathy took the cup from Julie whilst fluttering her eyelashes at Steve.

Turning to his secretary, he said, 'I have a few more letters for you to type, please.' He handed her a pile of files and a cassette.

'Thank you.' She smiled at the prospect: his smooth, deep voice on the cassettes always brightened her day.

Julie had developed a crush on Steve, but—comparing herself with the other secretaries—she doubted he would ever be interested in her romantically. Linda was a part-time model as well as a part-time secretary; her long, blonde, hair was perfectly straight, and she usually wore designer suits that accentuated her curvy figure. Cathy also had model looks; her gorgeous brown hair was naturally curly, and so shiny it gave the impression she'd waltzed out of a shampoo commercial.

Both her colleagues wore make-up, whereas Julie never did. She felt quite plain in comparison.

At break time, Julie joined the other secretaries in the kitchen.

'I'll make the tea,' said Linda.

Julie went to the toilet.

'Jules is such a plain Jane,' opined Linda as she prepared the tea. 'Never wears make-up, and never does anything to her hair—it just hangs.'

'I know.' Cathy nodded. 'And she's always wearing black, like no other colour has been invented. It's so depressing.'

'I'd be ashamed to wear her clothes,' snorted Linda. 'It looks like she gets them from a charity shop, or something.'

'She's only twenty-five but you'd think she was fifty.'

'True. And those glasses. Oh, my God; they don't suit her.'

Julie walked back into the room.

'I've made your tea, Jules,' said Linda.

'Thanks.'

Julie had overheard them. The toilets were next door to the kitchen, so it was easy enough to hear everything they said. It wasn't the first time she'd heard them talking about her. She tried not to take their comments to heart, but sometimes it made her sad.

Steve walked in. 'Hello, girls.' He smiled at them, and they all stared at him with dopey grins on their faces.

'Ooh,' breathed Linda when he'd returned to his office after pouring a coffee, 'he looks like the man from the Diet Coke adverts.'

'Yeah, I wish I was his secretary,' said Cathy. 'You're so lucky, Julie.'

Later in the afternoon, Linda approached Julie's desk.

'Jules, me and Cathy are going to The Starlight tonight; do you wanna come for a couple of drinks and a boogie? It'll be fun.'

'I'm not really in the mood, but thanks. Maybe another time.'

'The Starlight?' said Steve, who was now standing in his office doorway. 'I've never been there, but I've heard the music's good.'

Linda and Cathy grinned at each other, their eyes wide with delight.

'Yeah, it's great there. Me and Cathy go quite often,' gushed Linda. 'Do you want to come with us, Steve?'

'It's a date!' he said brightly.

Julie could only look on agape, wishing she'd agreed to join them.

*

Julie noticed the time on the clock above the fireplace in her living room: eight o'clock. Steve, Linda, and Cathy were probably at The Starlight club now. She felt sick to her stomach to think that one of those bitchy women might soon be Steve's new girlfriend. They were both crazy about him and both beautiful... It was only a matter of time.

She stood up and studied her reflection in the mirror above the sofa. *Why didn't I go with them?* She shook her head, realising Linda and Cathy would be dressed up to the nines in designer clothes with their perfect hair and make-up. *Steve wouldn't have noticed me, anyway.*

Julie trundled up the stairs to her bedroom, a dark mood descending.

*

Linda, Cathy, and Steve sauntered into The Starlight together. Steve went to buy them a round of drinks.

'May the best woman win,' said Linda, high-fiving Cathy and simultaneously admiring Steve as he made his way to the bar.

'He's mine,' said Cathy.

'I saw him first,' countered Linda, giggling.

'That's unfair; I can't help it if I was off sick on the day he started work.'

'He's mine,' teased Linda. 'God, he's gorgeous.'

'I can't believe we're here with him,' effused Cathy.

'Me neither.'

They turned their attention to Steve and observed that he was chatting with a woman at the bar.

'One of us should've gone to the bar with him, Linda. We can't let him chat up other women.'

'I'll go and interrupt them,' said Linda, walking away.

'Hi, Steve, have you got our drinks yet?' asked Linda pointedly, glaring at the striking woman seated next to him at the bar.

The woman avoided eye contact with Linda.

'Here you are.' Steve handed over the two cocktails. 'You can take Cathy's too.' He grinned, then stepped off the bar stool and ushered Linda a few feet away. 'Sorry, but I've met this girl and she's really nice.' He winked. 'I'm sure you and Cathy will have a great time on your own.'

He walked back to the woman with the flowing blonde curls and sequined low-cut dress.

Linda made her way to where Cathy was seated, looking glum.

'What's wrong, Linda?'

'That bloody girl, that's what. She's wearing so much make-up she might as well be a circus clown, but men are so bloody dumb. Her cleavage is on show and his tongue's hanging out.'

'I want to see,' said Cathy, stepping off her stool and approaching the bar.

When she returned, her face had fallen. 'She's gorgeous; like a supermodel, or something.'

'I know. Just our luck she'd be in here tonight,' grumbled Linda, gulping down her drink in one go. 'Fancy getting drunk?'

Cathy downed her drink and nodded.

The next day, Cathy and Linda were late for work; both had hangovers.

Steve phoned in sick.

Linda and Cathy were gossiping all morning about the beautiful blonde who had seduced him at the club, and with whom they imagined he must be spending the day.

When it was time for a tea break, Julie joined them in the kitchen.

'How was your evening at The Starlight?' asked Julie.

'Can't remember much about it,' said Cathy, glancing at her and then at Linda.

Linda shrugged. 'Except Steve copping off with a supermodel.'

'Are those false nails?' asked Linda, noticing Julie's hands.

Julie's mouth fell open. After recovering her composure, she said, 'I... I thought I should start wearing nail varnish.'

'You should, and you should wear make-up. You've got strong features; a bit of colour would make you look stunning.'

'True,' agreed Cathy.

Julie blushed and took a sip of her tea.

'So, I bet Steve's still in bed with that supermodel this morning; what'd'ya think, Cath?'

'Hmm... probably.'

47

'Um... no, actually,' said Julie. 'He's had a bit of an accident.'

'Accident?' chorused Linda and Cathy, bemused smirks on their faces.

'Yes.' Julie nodded. She smiled and explained, 'I met him at The Starlight last night and we went out for a meal, but when we got back to his place and I took off my wig and contact lenses, he fell off the bed and bumped his head. He couldn't believe it was me. I thought it best he stay in bed this morning.'

# Birthday Boy

Victor was the manager of Maryland Plc, a supermarket on the high street. Although nearly sixty years of age, married, with children and grandchildren, he constantly flirted with the young shop assistants.

'It's disgusting,' said Jenna, a bakery assistant. 'Yesterday, he pinched Lisa's bum. She's only sixteen. The poor girl looked so embarrassed; she went bright red.'

'She's young enough to be his granddaughter,' said Betty from behind the fish counter.

'He took a photo of me with his mobile phone when I leaned over to get something from the floor the other day,' said Suzanna, a shelf-stacker. 'I had a short skirt on, and he showed me the photo and said it reminded him of an old picture of a woman tennis player that used to hang on his bedroom wall when he was a boy. He was practically salivating when he was looking at it. Ugh.'

'We've got to teach him a lesson.' Jenna rubbed her chin in thought.

'He had an affair with a twenty-year-old checkout girl last year and then fired her when she broke off their relationship,' chipped in Brenda—one of the bakery assistants. 'They used to have sex in the staff toilets, apparently.'

'We should report him to a tribunal,' suggested Betty. 'It's sexual discrimination.'

'Have you noticed how he only employs women?' said Brenda, arms folded.

'Must be a mid-life crisis,' said Jenna.

'I hate the way he's always staring and making suggestive comments,' grumbled Suzanna.

'Maybe we should give him a taste of his own medicine. I've got an idea.' Jenna tapped her nose.

It was Victor's sixtieth birthday the following week. The staff organised a surprise party for him in the supermarket after closing time. Jenna came up with the idea and kept her plans under wraps. Her colleagues were reluctant to donate any money towards his birthday gift, but she managed to collect a decent amount by promising them it would be worth it.

'Well, well, well,' said Victor, 'I wasn't expecting this, girls.' He smiled at Jenna, who handed him a glass of champagne.

'Nothing but the best for you, Vic.'

He leaned in and tried to plant a kiss on her lips, but she dodged it just in time.

'We've all chipped in and got a present for you, Vic,' said Brenda.

'Ooh, how exciting!' He walked over to Brenda and put an arm around her.

She pulled away from him.

Everyone looked at Jenna, curious to find out what the surprise was.

Jenna went to the staff room door and opened it to reveal a tall woman with long blonde hair. 'Victor, meet Joan.' Jenna grinned at Victor.

Joan strutted towards Victor in high heels, long spindly legs tanned to perfection.

Most of the staff were whispering in each other's ears, gawping, or scowling at Jenna.

'You must be Victor; The Birthday Boy,' said Joan in a seductive French accent, taking Victor by the hand.

He turned bright red and grinned. 'Yes, I am. Lovely to meet you, Joan.'

'Joan's a dancer,' explained Jenna. 'We thought it would be nice if she entertained you.'

Joan led Victor into the staff room.

He swivelled his head briefly to wink at his employees before closing the door.

'I'm so disappointed in you, Jenna. How could you?' fumed Brenda bitterly.

'Yeah, after everything we talked about,' complained Betty.

'You're encouraging him to be a dirty old man,' said Lisa.

'Is Joan a stripper?' asked Suzanna.

'Yes.' Jenna nodded. She began to laugh.

'I'm glad you think it's funny. You should be ashamed of yourself,' said Betty, red-faced. 'He's going to be worse than ever now.'

'Wait,' said Brenda excitedly, 'I know, have you invited his wife so she'll catch him with the stripper, maybe?'

'No... Not quite,' said Jenna.

Brenda frowned. 'Well then, what—'

Just then, the staff room door swung open and Victor ran out. His face was pale and he appeared to be almost frightened. He had no shirt on, but nevertheless ran straight out of the supermarket. It was the middle of winter.

Many of the girls gasped. Most were waiting for Jenna to explain.

'Wh-what happened?' asked Betty.

At that moment, a half-dressed man emerged from the staff room smiling at Jenna.

'I should explain,' said Jenna, taking in the bemused faces around her. 'Joan is actually John. He's a male stripper. I don't think Vic will be in the mood to flirt with any of us again after this.' She collapsed into laughter, followed shortly by the rest of the girls.

# Happy Anniversary

'How can you break something like that to her on your anniversary? It's twisted. Anniversaries are supposed to be happy occasions. Don't do it, Les.'

Les let out a sigh. 'What am I supposed to do? Celebrate, and pretend nothing's wrong?' He regretted telling Dennis. Why had he told him? Perhaps he'd been wanting someone to back him up and make the guilt disappear. Instead, all Dennis had done was reaffirm his torturous feelings.

Catching a glimpse of his reflection in the mirror above the bar, Les saw signs of the sleepless nights he'd endured: the tenseness in his jawline and the deep-set frown, the dark rings around his eyes.

'It's not the right time,' persisted Dennis. 'I don't know how you can even be considering it.'

The comment exacerbated Les's sense of blameworthiness. He bowed his head and leaned forward on the bar. 'I've got to tell her now. I can't go on like this.'

'But, Les—'

'I never planned it this way. I know it's bad timing, but surely it'd be worse if I let her believe everything's fine between us.'

'Yeah, but why today?'

'She's booked a table at a restaurant for this evening. She's making a big deal of it. I can't bear to carry on the charade.'

Les's mind went back to the day before, when Anna had announced that she'd taken care of the anniversary plans. 'You probably forgot it was our anniversary, didn't you?' she'd said, giggling. He knew her well enough to work out that the giggle was a cover for emotions she was not yet willing, or able, to confront. The shine in her eyes foretold a tear or two that she would probably wipe away surreptitiously. They were not happy tears: of that he was certain. The spectre of his other affairs perpetually hung between them.

'Why didn't you say anything when she told you she'd booked the restaurant?' enquired Dennis. 'It'll be ten times worse to break it to her in a public place.'

'She only told me she'd booked it yesterday. I tried to say something, but I couldn't find the words.' Les stared straight ahead, his eyes distant. 'She was so happy about it.'

'All the more reason not to tell her at the restaurant.'

Les recalled the look of lost hope he'd seen in Anna's eyes. Her behaviour of late screamed desperation; she seemed too eager to please, as if struggling to hold on to what was left of their relationship. Was that what had driven him into Amber's arms?

'Maybe I just shouldn't turn up to the restaurant,' mused Les, finishing off his beer.

'That's the best idea you've come up with so far, mate,' said Dennis.

Les smiled a sad smile. Wasn't it fairer to both of them, especially Anna, to stop giving false hope to a hopeless situation? Besides, he had a suspicion that Anna already knew he was seeing Amber. It would explain her "desperate" behaviour. He'd never been able to keep anything hidden from Anna.

It would be the end of an era. Although he didn't love Anna anymore, they had been married for seven years and shared some good memories.

'It strikes me as a bit sudden, if I'm being honest,' opined Dennis. 'How long have you known this Amber?'

'A couple of weeks.'

'And you're willing to throw away a seven-year marriage for her? Are you sure it's not a midlife crisis—or, what's that thing called? The seven-year itch?'

'It's not. I love Amber. As silly as it probably sounds to you, I love her. She's the one. I've never felt like this before, not even with Anna.'

'You must've loved Anna to have stayed with her for so long.'

'We've come close to splitting up a few times.' He realised it had become more of a companionship, both of them afraid to leave the other—too afraid to be alone.

'Think carefully before you make any decisions, Les.'

His friend's words shook Les from his reverie.

'You've known Amber for ten minutes. How can you be so sure she feels the same way about you?'

Gazing into his empty beer glass, Les said, 'Amber makes me feel alive. She's special. It's early days, but she's told me she finds me attractive. That's a start, isn't it?'

'Have you told her you're married?'

'Yes, of course.'

'Hmm... I wouldn't trust a woman who dates married men. Have you discussed what you both want from the relationship? Maybe she's dating you because you're unavailable, a safe bet for a no-strings relationship.'

'Me and Amber were straight with each other from the start. She wasn't happy to date me when I said I was married. I told her my marriage is over. If I leave Anna, I'm sure me and Amber can start seeing each other properly.'

Dennis shrugged and finished off his beer. 'Well, I like Anna, and I think you're making the wrong decision. She's a good woman. Don't get me wrong—I'm your friend and I'm here for you—but Anna has put up with a lot from you over the years. What about the affair you had with the hairdresser, Rena? I remember you telling me then that you were thinking of leaving Anna until Rena dumped you. Anna forgave you. It can't have been easy for her; you shouldn't take her for granted.'

'I love Amber,' countered Les while his conscience replayed the words Anna had screamed at him after finding out about his last affair: *You don't know what love is, Les. Believe me, you haven't got a clue.*

'It's your life, Les.' Dennis ordered another round of drinks.

When Les returned home, he found a card on the kitchen table from Anna. It was a navy blue card with the words "Happy Anniversary" on the front, and inside she'd written, *"See you at the restaurant, darling. Love, Anna XXX"*.

Letting out a sigh, Les went to the drinks cabinet in the living room and poured himself a glass of whisky. Glancing at his watch, he knew he should be leaving for the restaurant. It would take him an hour to get there. He sat on the sofa, reached over to the telephone and dialled Amber's number.

'Hi, Amber, it's me.'

'Hi, Les.'

'How do you fancy meeting up tonight, babe?'

There was silence on the line for a moment, then, 'Listen, Les, I think we should cool things for a while.'

'Wh-why? What do you mean?'

'I mean, I don't think we should see each other anymore.'

'B-but—'

'Sorry, Les.' She hung up.

Les sat on the sofa, numb. He'd almost risked everything for that girl, and she'd dumped him without an explanation. Rage began to bubble inside him. He picked up the phone and redialled her number. No reply. He tried again; this time the engaged tone taunted him.

After downing his whisky, he stood up. From the corner of his eye he saw the anniversary card Anna had given him, which he'd brought with him from the kitchen. Sitting back down on the sofa, he picked up the card and reread it. Then he stared at it for a while, remembering all the good times they'd shared. *She really loves me.* Feeling remorseful, he realised it was always him who strayed. In seven years of marriage, she'd not so much as looked at another man. He recalled his friend's words: *"...you shouldn't take her for granted."*

On the way to the restaurant, Les bought a bunch of red roses and a box of Anna's favourite chocolates. In his mind, he could see her face, so full of joy about booking the restaurant for their anniversary. Perhaps among the hidden tears, she'd also held out hope that this romantic dinner would reawaken some spark between them. He knew he was to blame for making her doubt his loyalty. Tonight he had a chance to make amends. A smile came to his lips.

Walking into the restaurant, he spotted her straight away.

As he approached the table, it struck him that he'd not taken the time to notice her these past few years. He thought she looked more beautiful than ever and felt lucky to be her husband. After kissing her on the cheek, he gave her the roses and the chocolates. 'There you go, a box of your favourite chocolates.'

'They were my favourites until I found out I'm intolerant to milk.'

Les sat down. 'Oh, no. I forgot.'

'Don't worry,' she said, with a giggle.

'I should have got you the dark chocolate. Sorry.'

'It's fine,' she said.

There was that look again; the painted smile and the eyes holding back tears.

She placed the roses and chocolates on an empty chair to the side of the table.

Les's faux pas was soon forgotten as they set about ordering their meal. They chatted about the weather and their respective days at work until the waiter brought their food to the table.

They ate their meals in relative silence, the uncomplicated silence that comes from living with someone for years.

'I wanted this to be a very special evening,' said Anna, finishing off an indulgent chocolate dessert.

'It certainly is, darling. Thank you,' he said, raising his champagne glass. 'You must've taken out a bank loan to afford this place. The prices are extortionate.' He laughed.

'I had planned this as something we can remember for a long time.'

He smiled, but then noticed that her face appeared stern; it made him feel uneasy.

'Seven years.' A frown creased her brow. 'Some murderers serve less time.'

He laughed nervously.

'I wish it didn't have to end this way, Les.'

He nearly spilt his drink. 'Uh, end? Wh-what?'

'Our marriage is over. Let's face it.'

'You're breaking up with me?' His eyes widened.

'I'd hoped we could say goodbye on friendly terms.'

'Huh!' he fumed. 'Actually, I was going to break up with you this evening.' He stood up.

'I know,' she said in a calm voice, unperturbed.

'Y-you know?'

'I know about Amber.'

'H-how? Who told you?'

Anna calmly sipped some more champagne.

Sitting down, he leaned towards her. 'Look, I can explain. It was a mistake. Me and Amber are over. I love you. I've been a fool. We can work it out.'

'I wanted to give you another chance, I did, after all the affairs.'

'All? There were only a couple—'

'My friend Amber helped me decide.'

'What?'

'Amber agreed to take part in a little experiment—to see if I could still trust you, whether the marriage was worth saving. I was right, though; I can't trust you. We can't go on living a lie.' Standing up, Anna took her coat and handbag from the chair then leaned over and picked up the box of chocolates that he'd given her. 'I'll give these to Amber; she's earned them.'

'But, darling—' Les stood up.

'I'll leave you to settle the bill, shall I?' She smiled sweetly as she walked away.

**More books by Maria Savva:**

*Short story collections:*

Pieces of a Rainbow
Love and Loyalty (And Other Tales)
Fusion
Delusion and Dreams
3
Far Away In Time

(More short stories by Maria can be found in the BestsellerBound Anthologies, Volumes 1-4, and The Mind's Eye Series - Perspectives (book 1), Reflections (book 2), Triptychs (book 3), and Tales From The Cacao Tree (book 4).

*Novella:*

Cutting The Fat (co-author Jason McIntyre)

*Novels:*

Coincidences
A Time to Tell
Second Chances
The Dream
Haunted


Maria's Official Website: http://www.mariasavva.com